Christmas Carols

Selected and arranged by Karl Schulte
Illustrated by J. Ellen Dolce

The musical arrangements for "Goodnight King Wenceslas," "O Christmas Tree," "The Twelve Days of Christmas," and "Jingle Bells" are from *Favorite Christmas Carols* and are reprinted by permission of Simon & Schuster, Inc. © 1957 Simon & Schuster, Inc., and Artists and Writers Guild, Inc.

A GOLDEN BOOK • NEW YORK
Western Publishing Company, Inc., Racine, Wisconsin 53404

© 1993, 1990, 1942 Western Publishing Company, Inc. All rights reserved. Printed in the U.S.A. No part of this book may be reproduced or copied in any form without written permission from the publisher. All trademarks are the property of Western Publishing Company, Inc. Library of Congress Catalog Card Number: 81-80614   ISBN: 0-307-02979-4   MCMXCIV

Away in a Manger

Martin Luther

German Folk-Song

1. A - way in a man - ger, no crib for a bed, The lit - tle Lord Je - sus laid down His sweet head; The stars in the sky Looked down where He lay, The lit - tle Lord Je - sus, A - sleep on the hay.

2. The cat - tle are low - ing, the poor Ba - by wakes, But lit - tle Lord Je - sus no cry - ing He makes, I love Thee, Lord Je - sus! Look down from the sky, And stay by my cra - dle, Till morn - ing is nigh.

3. Be near me, Lord Je - sus, I ask Thee to stay, Close by me for - ev - er, and love me, I pray; Bless all the dear chil - dren in Thy ten - der care, And take us to heav - en, To live with Thee there.

O Thou Joyful Day

Words traditional

Sicilian Hymn

O thou joy-ful day, O thou bless-ed day, Glad-some,

peace-ful Christ-mas-tide.

1. Earth's hopes a - wak - en, Christ life hath
2. Christ's light is beam-ing, Our souls re-
3. King of all glo - ry, We bow be-

tak - en,
deem - ing, } Praise Him, O praise Him on ev-'ry side.
fore Thee,

I Heard the Bells on Christmas Day

Henry W. Longfellow

J. Baptiste Calkin

1. I heard the bells on Christ - mas day Their old fa - mil - iar ca - rols play, And wild and sweet the words re - peat Of peace on earth, good will to men.
2. I thought how, as the day had come, The bel - fries of all Christ - en - dom Had roll'd a - long th'un - bro - ken song Of peace on earth, good will to men.
3. And in de - spair I bow'd my head; "There is no peace on earth," I said, "For hate is strong, and mocks the song Of peace on earth, good will to men."
4. Then pealed the bells more loud and deep: "God is not dead, nor doth he sleep; The wrong shall fail, the right pre - vail, With peace on earth, good will to men."
5. Till ring - ing, sing - ing on its way, The world re - volved from night to day, A voice, a chime, a chant sub - lime, Of peace on earth, good will to men.

Joy to the World

Isaac Watts

George F. Handel

1. Joy to the world! the Lord is come; Let earth re-
2. Joy to the earth! the Sav-ior reigns; Let men their
3. No more let sins and sor-rows grow, Nor thorns in-
4. He rules the world with truth and grace, And makes the

ceive her King; Let ev-'ry heart pre-pare Him room,
songs em-ploy; While fields and floods, rocks, hills and plains
fest the ground; He comes to make His bless-ings flow
na-tions prove The glo-ries of His right-eous-ness,

And heav'n and na-ture sing, And heav'n and na-ture
Re-peat the sound-ing joy, Re-peat the sound-ing
Far as the curse is found, Far as the curse is
And won-ders of His love, And won-ders of His
(1.) And heav'n and na-ture sing, And

sing, And heav'n, and heav'n and na-ture sing.
joy, Re-peat, re-peat the sound-ing joy.
found, Far as, far as the curse is found.
love, And won-ders, and won-ders of His love.
heav'n and na-ture sing,

Deck the Halls

Traditional Welsh Melody

Words traditional

With spirit

1. Deck the halls with boughs of hol - ly,} Fa, la, la, la, la, la, la, la, la.
2. See the blaz - ing Yule be - fore us,} Fa, la, la, la, la, la, la, la, la.
3. Fast a - way the old year pass - es,}

'Tis the sea - son to be jol - ly,} Fa, la, la, la, la, la, la, la, la.
Strike the harp and join the cho - rus,}
Hail the new, ye lads and lass - es,}

Don we now our gay ap - par - el,} Fa, la, la, la, la, la, la, la, la.
Fol - low me in mer - ry meas - ure,}
Sing we joy - ous all to - geth - er,}

Troll the an - cient Yule - tide car - ol,} Fa, la, la, la, la, la, la, la, la.
While I tell of Yule - tide treas - ure,}
Heed - less of the wind and weath - er,}

Silent Night

Joseph Mohr
Translation anonymous

Franz Gruber

1. Si - lent night, Ho - ly night, All is calm, all is bright,
2. Si - lent night, Ho - ly night, Shep - herds quake at the sight.
3. Si - lent night, Ho - ly night, Son of God, love's pure light

'Round yon Vir - gin Moth - er and Child, Ho - ly In - fant so ten-der and mild,
Glo - ries stream from heav - en a - far, Heav'n - ly hosts sing Al - le - lu - ia;
Ra - diant beams from Thy ho - ly face, With the dawn of re - deem - ing grace,

Sleep in heav - en - ly peace, Sleep in heav - en - ly peace.
Christ the Sa - vior is born, Christ the Sa - vior is born.
Je - sus, Lord, at Thy birth, Je - sus, Lord, at Thy birth.

Jingle Bells

Tune by James Pierpont

Arranged by Norman Lloyd

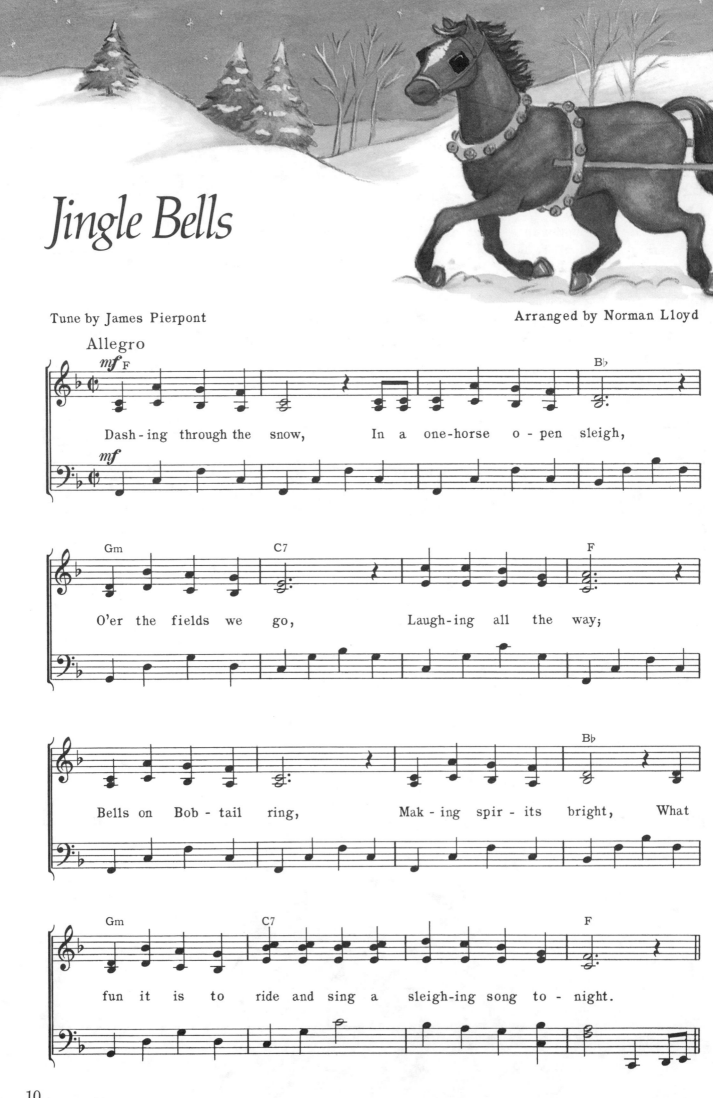

Dash - ing through the snow, In a one-horse o - pen sleigh,

O'er the fields we go, Laugh - ing all the way;

Bells on Bob - tail ring, Mak - ing spir - its bright, What

fun it is to ride and sing a sleigh-ing song to - night.

CHORUS

Jin - gle bells, Jin - gle bells, Jin - gle all the way!

Oh, what fun it is to ride in a one-horse o - pen sleigh!

Jin - gle bells, Jin - gle bells, Jin - gle all the way!

Oh, what fun it is to ride in a one-horse o - pen sleigh!

Angels From the Realms of Glory

James Montgomery

Henry Smart

1. An - gels, from the realms of glo - ry, Wing your flight o'er all the earth; Ye, who sang cre - a - tion's sto - ry, Now pro - claim Mes - si - ah's birth:
2. Shep - herds in the field a - bid - ing, Watch - ing o'er your flocks by night; God with man is now re - sid - ing, Yon - der shines the in - fant light:
3. Sa - ges, leave your con - tem - pla - tions, Bright - er vis - ions beam a - far; Seek the great De - sire of na - tions, Ye have seen His na - tal star:

Come and wor - ship, Come and wor - ship, Wor - ship Christ, the new - born King.

O Come, All Ye Faithful

English translation by
Rev. Frederick Oakeley (1802-1880)

Latin Hymn of the 18th Century,
Attributed to John Reading

1. O come, all ye faith - ful, Joy - ful and tri - um - phant, O
2. Sing, choirs of an - gels, Sing in ex - ul - ta - tion,
3. Yea, Lord, we greet Thee, Born this hap - py morn - ing;

come ye, O come ye to Beth - le - hem, Come and be - hold Him
Sing, all ye cit - i - zens of heav'n a - bove: Glo - ry to God
Je - sus to Thee be glo - ry giv'n, Word of the Fa - ther

born the King of an - gels;
In the high - est; } O come let us a - dore Him, O
now in flesh ap - pear - ing;

come let us a - dore Him, O come let us a - dore Him, Christ the Lord.

God Rest Ye Merry, Gentlemen

Words traditional

Traditional English Melody

1. God rest ye mer - ry, gen-tle-men, Let noth-ing you dis - may, For
2. From God, our Heav-en-ly Fa-ther, A bless-ed an - gel came, And
3. The shep-herds at these ti - dings Re-joic-ed much in mind, And

Je - sus Christ, our Sa - vi - our, Was born up - on this day: To
un - to cer - tain shep - herds Brought ti - dings of the same: How
left their flocks a - feed - ing In tem-pest, storm and wind, And

save us all from Sa - tan's pow'r, When we were gone a - stray): O
that in Beth - le - hem was born The Son of God by name: O
went to Beth - le - hem straight-way, The Bless - ed Babe to find: O

ti - dings of com-fort and joy, Com-fort and joy, O ti - dings of com-fort and joy.

The First Nowell

Words traditional

Traditional English Melody
Harmonized by Sir John Stainer

1. The first Now - ell the an-gel did say Was to cer-tain poor
2. They look - ed up and saw a star Shin-ing in the
3. This star drew nigh to the north - west, O'er Beth - le -
4. Then en - ter'd in those wise - men three, Full rev - 'rent-

shep-herds in fields as they lay; In fields where they lay keep-ing their
East, be - yond them far, And to the earth it gave great
hem it took its rest, And there it did both stop and
ly up - on their knee, And of - fer'd there, in His pres-

sheep, On a cold win-ter's night that was so deep.
light, And so it con-tin-ued both day and night.
stay Right o-ver the place where Je-sus lay. Now - ell, Now-
ence, Their gold and myrrh and frank-in-cense.

ell, Now-ell, Now-ell, Born is the King of Is-ra-el.

Hark! The Herald Angels Sing

Charles Wesley

Mendelssohn

Good King Wenceslas

Traditional

Arranged by Norman Lloyd

1. Good King Wen - ces - las look'd out, On the feast of Ste - phen,
2. "Hith - er, page, and stand by me, If thou knows't it tell - ing,
3. "Bring me flesh, and bring me wine, Bring me pine - logs hith - er:
4. "Sire, the night is dark - er now, And the wind grows strong - er;
5. In his mas - ter's steps he trod, Where the snow lay dint - ed;

When the snow lay round - a - bout, Deep and crisp and e - ven.
Yon - der peas - ant, who is he? Where and what his dwell - ing?"
Thou and I shall see him dine, When we bear them thith - er."
Fails my heart I know not how; I can go no long - er."
Heat was in the ver - y sod Which the Saint had print - ed.

Bright - ly shone the moon that night, Though the frost was cru - el,
"Sire, he lives a good league hence, Un - der - neath the moun - tain,
Page and mon - arch, forth they went, Forth they went to - geth - er;
"Mark my foot - steps, my good page, Tread thou in them bold - ly;
There - fore, Chris - tian men, be sure, Wealth or rank pos - sess - ing,

When a poor man came in sight, Gath - 'ring win - ter fu - el.
Right a - gainst the for - est fence, By Saint Ag - nes' foun - tain."
Through the rude wind's wild la - ment And the bit - ter weath - er.
Thou shalt find the win - ter's rage Freeze thy blood less cold - ly."
Ye who now will bless the poor, Shall your - selves find bless - ing.

The Holly and the Ivy

Words traditional

Old French Melody

1. The hol - ly and the i - vy, Now both are full well grown, Of
2. The hol - ly bears a blos - som, As white as an - y flow'r, And
3. The hol - ly bears a ber - ry, As red as an - y blood, And
4. The hol - ly bears a prick - le, As sharp as an - y thorn, And

all the trees with - in the wood, The hol - ly bears the crown.
Ma - ry bore sweet Je - sus Christ, To be our sweet Sa - vior.
Ma - ry bore sweet Je - sus Christ, To do poor sin - ners good.
Ma - ry bore sweet Je - sus Christ, On Christ - mas Day in the morn.

O the ris - ing of the sun, The run - ning of the deer, The play - ing of the

mer - ry or - gan, Sweet sing - ing in the choir, Sweet sing - ing in the choir.

O Christmas Tree

Traditional German Tune

Arranged by Norman Lloyd

1. O Christ-mas Tree, O Christ-mas Tree, Your branch-es green de - light us. O Christ-mas Tree, O Christ-mas Tree, Your branch-es green de - light us. They're green when sum - mer days are bright; They're green when win - ter snow is white. O

2. O Christ-mas Tree, O Christ-mas Tree, You give us so much pleas-ure! O Christ-mas Tree, O Christ-mas Tree, You give us so much pleas - ure! How oft at Christ - mas - tide the sight, O green fir tree, gives us de - light! O

Christ-mas Tree, O Christ-mas Tree, Your branch-es green de - light us.
Christ-mas Tree, O Christ-mas Tree, You give us so much pleas-ure!

O Little Town of Bethlehem

Phillips Brooks

Lewis H. Redner

1. O lit - tle town of Beth - le - hem! How still we see thee lie; A-bove thy deep and dream-less sleep The si - lent stars go by; Yet in thy dark streets shin - eth The ev - er - last - ing Light; The hopes and fears of all the years Are met in thee to - night.

2. For Christ is born of Ma - ry; And gath - er'd all a - bove, While mor-tals sleep, the an - gels keep Their watch of won-d'ring love. O morn-ing stars, to - geth - er Pro - claim the ho - ly birth! And prais-es sing to God the King, And peace to men on earth.

3. How si - lent - ly, how si - lent - ly, The won - drous gift is giv'n! So God im-parts to hu - man hearts The bless - ings of His heav'n. No ear may hear His com - ing, But in this world of sin, Where meek souls will re - ceive Him still The dear Christ en - ters in.

4. O ho - ly Child of Beth - le - hem! De - scend to us, we pray; Cast out our sins, and en - ter in, Be born in us to - day. We hear the Christ-mas an - gels The great glad ti - dings tell, O come to us, a - bide with us; Our Lord Em - man - u - el!

It Came Upon the Midnight Clear

The Twelve Days of Christmas

Traditional English

Arranged by Norman Lloyd

1. On the first day of Christ-mas, my true love sent to me, A par-tridge in a pear tree. ____ 2. On the se-cond day of Christ-mas, my true love sent to me, two tur-tle doves and a par-tridge in a pear tree. 3. On the third day of Christ-mas, my true love sent to me, three French hens,

two tur-tle doves, and a par-tridge in a pear tree. 4. On the

fourth day of Christ-mas, my true love sent to me, four call-ing birds,
three French hens,

two tur-tle doves, and a par-tridge in a pear tree. 5. On the

fifth day of Christ-mas, my true love sent to me five, gold rings,

four call-ing birds, three French hens, two tur-tle doves, and a

par-tridge in a pear tree.___ 6. On the sixth day of Christ-mas my
7. On the seventh day — *etc.*

Gm   C7   F   F   Gm   Am   G7

true love sent to me,   six   geese   a - lay - ing, *(to 5*   five gold
                           seven swans   a - swim - ming, *(to 6)*
                           eight maids   a - milk - ing, *(to 7)*
                           nine   la - dies danc - ing, *(to 8)*
                           ten   lords   a - leap - ing, *(to 9)*
                           eleven pi - pers pi - ping, *(to 10)*
                           twelve drum - mers drum - ming, *(to 11)*

C   F   Bb   C7

rings,   four call-ing birds, three French hens,   two tur-tle doves, and a

F   Bb F   C7   F   *D. S.*

par - tridge in a pear tree. ___

What Child Is This?

Words traditional

Traditional English Tune, "Greensleeves"
Harmonized by Sir John Stainer

1. What Child is this, Who, laid to rest, On Ma-ry's lap is sleep-ing?Whom
2. Why lies He in such mean es-tate, Where ox and ass are feed-ing? Good
3. So bring Him in-cense, gold and myrrh, Come peas-ant, king, to own Him, The

an-gels greet with an-thems sweet,While shep-herds watch are keep-ing?
Chris-tian, fear: for sin-ners here The si-lent Word is plead-ing:
King of kings sal-va-tion brings,Let lov-ing hearts en-throne Him.

This, this is Christ the King, Whom shep-herds guard and an-gels sing:
Nails, spear, shall pierce Him through,The Cross be borne, for me, for you:
Raise, raise the song on high, The Vir-gin sings her lul-la-by:

Haste, haste to bring Him laud, The Babe, the Son of Ma-ry!
Hail, hail the Word made flesh, The Babe, the Son of Ma-ry!
Joy, joy for Christ is born, The Babe, the Son of Ma-ry!

We Three Kings of Orient Are

John H. Hopkins   John H. Hopkins

All 1. We three kings of O - rient are; Bear - ing gifts we tra-verse a-
Melchior 2. Born a King on Beth-le-hem's plain, Gold I bring, to crown Him a-
Caspar 3. Frank-in-cense to of-fer have I, In-cense owns a De-i-ty
Balthazar 4. Myrrh is mine, its bit-ter per-fume Breathes a life of gath-er-ing
All 5. Glo-rious now be-hold Him a-rise, King and God and sac-ri-

far, Field and foun-tain, moor and moun-tain, Fol-low-ing yon-der star.
gain, King for-ev-er, ceas-ing nev-er, O-ver us all to reign.
nigh, Pray'r and prais-ing, all men rais-ing, Wor-ship Him, God most High.
gloom; Sor-row-ing, sigh-ing, bleed-ing, dy-ing, Seal'd in the stone-cold tomb.
fice; Al-le-lu-ia, Al-le-lu-ia, Earth to the heav'ns re-plies.

CHORUS

O star of won-der, star of night, Star with roy-al beau-ty bright,

West-ward lead-ing, still pro-ceed-ing, Guide us to Thy per-fect light.